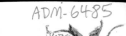

Mimosa

and

the River of Wisdom

J. H. Sweet

Illustrated by Holly Sierra

SOURCEBOOKS
Jabberwocky
AN IMPRINT OF SOURCEBOOKS

Published by Sourcebooks Jabberwocky, an imprint of Sourcebooks, Inc.

P.O. Box 4410, Naperville, Illinois 60567-4410
(630) 961-3900
Fax: (630) 961-2168
www.sourcebooks.com

Library of Congress Cataloging-in-Publication Data

Sweet, J. H.
    Mimosa and the River of Wisdom / J.H. Sweet.
        p. cm.
    "The Fairy Chronicles."
    Summary: While personally debating whether to use her fairy magic to help her mother stop smoking which would cost her, her fairy spirit, Mimosa and her fairy friends are sent to find the librarian of the Library of the Ages who has disappeared.
    ISBN-13: 978-1-4022-1162-1 (pbk.)
    ISBN-10: 1-4022-1162-7 (pbk.)
    [1. Fairies—Fiction. 2. Magic—Fiction. 3. Conduct of life—Fiction.] I. Title.
    PZ7.S9547Mi 2008
    [Fic]—dc22
                                                    2007037138

Printed and bound in the United States of America.
IN 10 9 8 7 6 5 4 3 2 1

To Dad,
for wisdom

MEET THE

Mimosa

NAME:
Alexandra Hastings

FAIRY NAME AND SPIRIT:
Mimosa

WAND:
Emu Feather

GIFT:
Sensitive and understanding of
others' needs

MENTOR:
Evelyn Holstrom,
Madam Monarch

Spiderwort

NAME:
Jensen Fortini

FAIRY NAME AND SPIRIT:
Spiderwort

WAND:
Small, Brilliant Red
Cardinal Feather

GIFT:
Cleverness; the ability to come
up with good ideas and plans

MENTOR:
Godmother,
Madam Chameleon

FAIRY TEAM

Dewberry

Madam Monarch

NAME:
Lauren Kelley

NAME:
Evelyn Holstrom

FAIRY NAME AND SPIRIT:
Dewberry

FAIRY NAME AND SPIRIT:
Madam Monarch

WAND:
Single Strand of Braided
Unicorn Tail Hair

WAND:
Single, Gleaming
Dandelion Seed

GIFT:
Great knowledge and wisdom

GIFT:
Strength and endurance

MENTOR:
Grandmother,
Madam Goldenrod

MENTOR TO:
Marigold and Mimosa

Inside you is the power to do anything™

Come visit us at fairychronicles.com

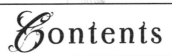

Contents

Chapter One

A Dilemma

Alexandra Hastings was waiting for her friend, Vinca Simpson, to come over to play. With one more week of summer vacation still left, Alexandra hoped to eke out every bit of summer fun possible before returning to school. She sat on her living room couch and fingered a tiny, square silver box about the size of a sugar cube.

The box had a midnight-blue ribbon encircling it in both directions, as though it were wrapped like a present. Where the ribbon was tied in a bow on the top of the box, there was a small clasp. Alexandra slipped a long, fine silver chain through the clasp and placed the pendant around her neck.

The silver box had a very special meaning. Alexandra had received it as a gift earlier in the summer, when she and her friends participated in a daring adventure to help save all of mankind from torment and misery.

In addition to being like other ten-year-old girls, Alexandra and many of her friends were also fairies; and fairies were tasked with the important job of protecting nature and fixing serious problems. The last fairy adventure had involved traveling to the Island of Shadows, meeting with the King and Queen of Shadowland, helping a gryphon defeat an evil chimera and the Demon of Light, and recovering several stolen human shadows.

Human beings cannot survive without their shadows, so the success of their mission was very important. The king and queen appreciated the fairies' help very much and rewarded the girls with gifts of tiny silver boxes that were normally used to deliver shadows to newborn babies.

The gift box did not contain a shadow because Alexandra already had hers, attached to her since birth. Instead, it was filled with beautiful, sparkling black sand from the shores of the Island of Shadows. Even though the mission had been a little scary, the adventure had also been exciting, and Alexandra remembered the journey to the island fondly.

Alexandra was a mimosa fairy, inhabited by the fairy spirit of a mimosa tree blossom. She had long, straight blond hair and bright blue eyes. In the standard fairy form of six inches, Mimosa had tall, wispy pink wings and wore a glistening dress made of silky mimosa flower strands in colors of light pink, white, peach, and dark pink. Her dress came to just above her knees, and she wore soft pink slippers and a belt to match. On her belt, she carried her fairy wand, a small pouch of pixie dust, and the fairy handbook.

Mimosa's wand was a small, brownish-gray emu feather that was forked and curled on both tips. The feather was enchanted to help her perform fairy magic. The glittering pixie dust in her pouch was also used for fairy magic. And the handbook contained answers to fairy questions and advice to help her make good fairy decisions. It was also an interactive book that aged with its fairy owner.

Young fairies were not allowed to use fairy magic without approval from their mentors. Madam Monarch, who was blessed with a monarch butterfly fairy spirit, was Mimosa's mentor. Mimosa had only inherited Madam Monarch as her mentor upon moving to Texas from Montana in the spring, when her mother was transferred with her job. Mrs. Hastings was raising her daughter by herself since Mimosa's father had died in a car accident when Mimosa was four.

Mimosa's mother didn't know that her daughter was a fairy, and fairy activities had to be kept secret because it would be hard for parents to understand why their daughters had to be away from home sometimes on dangerous fairy missions. Regular people could not even recognize fairies when they saw them because to non-magical people, fairies only appeared to look like their fairy spirits.

Madam Monarch didn't need to teach Mimosa very much because her previous mentor, Madam Gooseberry, had done such a good job. However, all young fairies needed to be supervised because being a

fairy was a tremendous responsibility. To be blessed with power, and to gain the maturity and wisdom to know how to use the gift properly, took some guidance. So a mentor was assigned.

When Mimosa first moved to Texas, she told her new fairy friends all about the fairies in Montana. There were less flower fairies in Montana and more berry fairies, along with herb, insect, and bat fairies. Her new friends didn't believe her at first, that there really were bat fairies, until they looked up types of fairies in the fairy handbook.

Mimosa's fairy handbook was a different color than those of her friends. Hers was a pale, sky blue color since it originated in Montana; whereas, all of the native Texas fairies carried handbooks of a fawn tan color. When she looked up types of fairies, this is the information the handbook shared:

Types of Fairy Spirits: Fairies derive their spirits from numerous sources. Some of the more common spirits come from flowers, berries, herbs, and tree blossoms. Fairy spirits can also come from insects like dragonflies, bees, butterflies, moths, fireflies, and beetles. There are also fairies whose spirits come from small birds, animals, lizards, amphibians, and sea creatures such as finches, robins, wrens, sparrows, moles, shrews, bats, sea horses, starfish, oysters, salamanders, and toads.

After the handbook confirmed the information, the other fairies did indeed believe that there were bat fairies. And it made sense. There was a chameleon fairy and a toad fairy right in this region. Madam Toad, the current leader of the

Southwest region of fairies, was a very old, wise, and well-known fairy. The girls also knew that Madam Shrew was leader of the fairies for the far North region, and Madam Oyster led the fairies in the Gulf region. The young fairies were hopeful that maybe, one day, they would get to meet a bat fairy.

The fairies of the Southwest region all met together frequently at Fairy Circles, which were gatherings of fairies. They met for fairy celebrations and to discuss important problems and plan ways to fix them. Mimosa and Vinca, who was a periwinkle fairy, would be attending a Fairy Circle later in the week.

Each fairy was given a special gift relating to her fairy spirit. Mimosa's gift included enhanced sensitivity, understanding, and caring of others. She was a good listener and had the ability to empathize. With these qualities, she gave exceptional advice that was full of clarity and wisdom. Mimosa was already planning to be a counselor when she grew up, either a school counselor or a professional therapist.

Mimosa had received a nut message from Periwinkle the day before to arrange to play this afternoon. Nut messages were hollowed-out nuts that fairies used to send notes to one another. Animals and birds usually delivered the messages.

The Hastings' neighbor, Mrs. Welch, looked after Mimosa during the summer while her mother was at work. Mrs. Welch was watching television in the living room when Periwinkle arrived, as expected. The girls shut themselves into Mimosa's bedroom so they wouldn't disturb Mrs. Welch, and so they wouldn't be overheard. Mimosa had a very important problem that she wanted to discuss with Periwinkle.

Periwinkle was adopted after losing both of her parents at age five. She too

understood what it was like to lose someone very close, so the girls had a special
bond.

As a fairy, Periwinkle wore a bright
pink periwinkle petal dress; and she had
tiny, pale pink wings. Her wand was an
elephant's eyelash, and her special fairy
gift was the ability to channel energy
from the sun.

Periwinkle was the only Native American fairy in the region so far. Her mother
had been a Cherokee Indian. Because of
her heritage, Periwinkle had many
qualities relating to the Native American
culture. She didn't get lost in the woods
because she could tell directions without a
compass. And she could recognize various
animal tracks and edible plants.

She also had a spirit guide who took the
form of a small snail and most often rode
on her shoulder. Periwinkle was the only
one who could see her tiny companion. He

gave her advice as needed to help her make good decisions.

As they sat on the bed together, Mimosa sighed and tried to word her thoughts carefully. Periwinkle pulled her long dark hair back into a ponytail, clasping it with a stretchy hair tie, as she watched her friend's face closely, waiting for her to speak.

After a few moments, Mimosa sighed again, then finally said, "I'm really worried about my mom. She has tried so hard to quit smoking, but she can't. I want to help her."

"What do you mean, help her?" asked Periwinkle, hesitantly.

"Well..." said Mimosa. "You know...a little fairy help."

"But you can't!" Periwinkle cried loudly. She glanced at the door and lowered her voice. "You know that we can't use fairy magic to solve personal problems. You could lose your fairy spirit."

The girls sat together not speaking for a while. Periwinkle looked at her spirit guide. He shook his head. At this time, he had no wise words for her.

After several minutes, Mimosa spoke again. "I'm just so frustrated for her. She has tried everything to stop. And I see the struggle in her face. She is desperate to quit. She knows that she needs to, for both of us." Mimosa's voice was shaking, and she couldn't continue. A lump in her throat was choking her, and she started crying. Periwinkle hugged her friend tightly, but didn't have an answer for her.

When Mimosa was able to speak again, she told Periwinkle, "I talked to Jensen last week." (Jensen Fortini was a spiderwort herb fairy, and was one of the best fairies for solving problems and coming up with good plans.) "She couldn't think of a solution either," Mimosa added.

The girls played cat's cradle and jacks for a while and talked about things like the upcoming Fairy Circle, what books they were reading, boys, starting school next week, and new clothes.

When Periwinkle left an hour later, she urged her friend not to do any thing rash. "Think carefully about anything you might be planning to do. Consult Madam Monarch if you need to. This is very important."

Mimosa nodded as she said goodbye to her friend. But she was even more frustrated. There didn't seem to be a solution to her problem, other than getting into trouble if she used fairy magic.

For the rest of the afternoon and evening, Mimosa tried to read, watch television, and do a crossword puzzle. But she was very upset and worried.

Just before bedtime, her mother came in to say goodnight. They talked for a while, about little things. This was the most special time of day for both of them. The apartment was quiet, with no distractions, and it was a very secure and calming time to share things.

As she was trying to get to sleep, Mimosa heard her mother go out onto the balcony to smoke a cigarette. She sat up in bed, hot tears rolling down her face. Considering all of the things her mother had tried so far to stop smoking over the last couple of years, it seemed hopeless that she would ever be able to actually manage to quit on her own.

Mimosa was so upset about this that she did something very impulsive next. She pulled out her emu feather wand, gave it a furious wave, and said, *"Disappear cigarettes!"* With the exception of the one her mother was smoking, all of the cigarettes in the apartment vanished, including the ones in her mother's purse and two full cartons in the kitchen cabinet.

Mimosa didn't feel any better after she had performed the spell. The action hadn't solved anything, and she knew that she was going to get in a lot of trouble, both with her mother and with her fairy mentor. She felt terrible, and it took a long time, but she finally cried herself to sleep.

Chapter Two

The Warning

The scolding began before breakfast even. Before the milk was even on the cereal, Mrs. Hastings sat her daughter down, looked deeply into her eyes, and sighed exasperatedly. "I am very upset with you, Alexandra. You know that I am trying to quit smoking?" Mimosa nodded glumly, but didn't say anything.

Her mother sighed again, then added, "Throwing away my cigarettes is not going to help me stop smoking, and they are very expensive. Promise me you won't do it again." Mimosa nodded once more.

Then her mother told her, "Ms. Holstrom called last night after you had gone to bed. Apparently, there's a Girls Club event she forgot to tell you about. She'll be picking you up at nine o'clock. I've half a mind to keep you home, but Evelyn stressed that this is the last meeting for awhile since school will be starting next week."

Mimosa was not surprised at all about the meeting scheduled for today. Evelyn Holstrom was none other than Madam Monarch, and there was very little chance that either of them would be participating in a Girls Club activity today. Mimosa knew that the meeting was going to be about her inappropriate use of fairy magic last night.

Mimosa's mother gave her a hug and kiss goodbye, telling her, "We'll talk more tonight. And I promise I will try the patches again." Mimosa nodded, but didn't feel too enthused about her mother's promise since she had already tried the stop-smoking patches twice before. Mrs. Welch was just coming over from her apartment as Mimosa watched her mother disappear down the stairs and out the front door of the apartment building.

Madam Monarch arrived promptly at nine. She didn't say anything to Mimosa as they both buckled themselves up in her lime green station wagon. After they had driven a few blocks, Madam Monarch finally said, "We are going to see Madam Toad."

Mimosa nodded sadly, but couldn't say anything. The lump in her throat was back, and was about twice as large as the day before. She knew it was very likely that she was going to lose her fairy spirit.

They met with Madam Toad, whose real name was Mrs. Jenkins, at her house on Belvin Street. The house was a very large, three-story historic home, painted white,

with huge columns on either side of the porch steps. There was a beautiful flower garden on one side of the house and a gazebo on the other. Madam Toad had tea and cookies set out for them in her large sunny parlor, but Mimosa couldn't eat or drink anything. She just hung her head sadly and kept silent.

Madam Toad wasn't quite as foreboding in woman form as she was in fairy form. In fact, she smiled and spoke kindly to her. "First of all, Mimosa, your fairy spirit is not being taken from you today. You are being given a warning. However, we need to know why you used forbidden fairy magic. Madam Monarch and I both know that *you* know you cannot use fairy magic for these types of things."

Mimosa looked up at both Madam Monarch and Madam Toad. She was only slightly relieved not to have lost her fairy spirit because her will was very determined, and she knew she couldn't promise them that she wouldn't do something like this again.

When Mimosa spoke, her voice faltered, and sadness crept into her heart, just as it had when she was talking to Periwinkle the day before. "My mother has tried everything to stop smoking. She's tried gum, patches, herbs, prescription pills, and hypnosis. But she just can't do it. I want to help her. She can't do it alone." There was a desperate note in Mimosa's voice.

Madam Monarch spoke next, very softly. "Fairy powers cannot be used for these matters, even for a very good cause. Mother Nature is extremely firm on this." (Mother Nature was the supervisor of nature and the guardian of all magical creatures, including fairies.) Madam Monarch sighed heavily when she spoke again. "We would all like your mother to quit smoking, but she will have to find a way to accomplish this herself. If you try to help her again with magic, your fairy spirit will be taken from you. If you forfeit your fairy spirit, your memory will be wiped of all fairy knowledge. You will not remember that you were a fairy, or recall any of your fairy adventures. Also, your friends who are fairies will not be able to discuss fairy things with you."

Mimosa regained her voice and pleaded with the two older fairies. "Then what can I do?" she asked earnestly. "I have already lost my father. I don't want to lose my mother too. I've done volunteer work at nursing homes and at the hospital. I've seen what lung cancer does to people. There is so much pain, physical and emotional, both for the sick person and their families." Her voice was shaking again, and tears flowed freely down her face. Sitting next to Mimosa on the couch, Madam Monarch hugged her very tightly and rocked her back and forth gently.

After several minutes, Madam Toad found her voice again. "I wish there was some way to make an exception, but there isn't. Hopefully, someday soon, there will be a cure for that type of addiction, so people can stop if they want to. Though I don't know how much emphasis there is on finding some kind of a cure for smoking addiction, since it is not illegal to smoke and it is a choice adults are free to make, even if smoking is bad for their health."

Madam Toad waited a few moments before speaking again. "We cannot use fairy magic to restore Hollyhock's hearing, even though we would like to."

Mimosa looked at Madam Toad closely, surprised by what she had just heard. Hollyhock was the only deaf fairy in their group. After a few moments, the young fairy shook her head a little in confusion, and asked, "*Would* fairy magic be able to give Hollyhock back her hearing?"

Madam Monarch and Madam Toad both looked at each other before responding. After a long pause, Madam Toad answered, "Yes. There is magic that can restore hearing to a deaf person. But we cannot use it unless the hearing loss was caused by the actions of a magical creature under Mother Nature's guardianship. You see, Mimosa, we can only fix things with magic when magic was involved in causing the problem."

Mimosa frowned, as Madam Toad continued. "Madam Oyster's husband is very ill. Magical blue moon clover might work as a cure for his illness, but it cannot be used. His illness was not caused by a magical creature's actions.

"And you know that fairies can only help clean up after natural disasters; we cannot use magic to prevent them. You must try to help your mother quit smoking using some non-magical means, like technology."

If anything, Mimosa felt worse after the meeting with Madam Monarch and Madam Toad. Even though she had not lost her fairy spirit, she was no closer to a solution than before. Mimosa and Madam Monarch were both silent on the drive home.

As she dropped Mimosa off, Madam Monarch said, "I'll pick you up at ten on Thursday for the Fairy Circle." She gave Mimosa a smile of encouragement; but underlying the smile, a worried expression was visible in her eyes and in the lines of her face.

Even though she had been mentoring Mimosa less than a year, Madam Monarch knew how determined the young fairy was. Mimosa's concern and caring for others gave her an inner strength of will—to help at all costs. Madam Monarch feared that this would build to a kind of tidal wave or avalanche that could not be stopped.

The fairy mentor drove away sadly, not knowing what else she could do. We all have to make tough decisions in our lives and live with the consequences. And Madam Monarch couldn't help but admire Mimosa's dedication to her mother's well being.

Chapter Three

Prunella, the Witch

Mimosa sat cross-legged on her bed, holding her fairy handbook and thinking. She was desperate for a means to help her mother stop smoking, and her brain was doing all kinds of storming.

She thought again about all of the things her mother had tried. When her mind stopped on herbs, Mimosa suddenly thought, *Witches use herbs*. So she quickly looked up witches in her handbook:

Witches: Witches are magical beings of different types depending on the kind of magic they practice — light or dark. If at all possible, limit contact with witches to those that are light, because dark witches can be dangerous. Some witches concentrate on specialties such as healing, illusions, and predictions. Many witches are masters of developing magic seeds for purposes that include inducing sleep, inspiring love, causing invisibility, forcing truth, enhancing memory, and increasing energy.

"What about a stop-smoking magic seed?" Mimosa asked her handbook. The following words immediately appeared below the entry she had just read:

Yes, a witch can develop seeds that are specific to resisting addictions, including smoking.

In addition to answering her question, the handbook also addressed her directly:

Mimosa (Alexandra),
Turn to the first page of your handbook so we can talk.

She turned the pages reluctantly, knowing exactly what was coming. On the first page of her handbook, a question was written:

What are you thinking of doing?

A little frustrated, Mimosa answered the question. "Well, you were with me this morning when I got the warning. Can't you guess what I'm up to?"

The handbook took a long time to respond:

I just don't want you to make a hasty decision. I speak for your

*wand too in telling you that we
don't want to lose you. We don't
want to be assigned to anyone else.
We love you.*

Mimosa closed her handbook, hugging it tightly. The lump in her throat

now felt about ten times the size it was the day before.

Mrs. Welch gave the okay for Mimosa to take a short walk down the block to the park by herself. There were always a lot of other kids, some of them with their moms, at the park in the afternoons, and the route to and from the park was also safe to walk.

"I won't be more than an hour," she told Mrs. Welch.

However, Mimosa didn't make it all the way to the park. Instead, she stopped three houses down from the apartment building where she lived. Looking into Mr. Johnson's yard, she spotted what she was looking for. Mr. Hempell, the garden gnome, was furiously weeding a row of peppers with a tiny hoe. Dirt was flying in all directions from his war with the weeds, and it was clear that Mr. Hempell was winning this battle.

Like all garden gnomes, Mr. Hempell was about ten inches high and a dusty

brown color all over. He wore overalls with fifteen pockets full of tools, seeds, bulbs, and roots; and he had a large, bushy moustache.

Because of gnome disguise magic, regular people couldn't see gnomes. In fact, if Mr. Johnson were to look out into his garden right now, all he would see was a large aluminum watering can where Mr. Hempell stood. However, since Mimosa was a fairy, she could see Mr. Hempell as a gnome.

Mimosa called to him through the fence. "Mr. Hempell! May I speak with you for a minute?"

The gnome came trotting across the garden furrows very quickly, happy for a break. "Hello, Mimosa. Nice day for a walk."

They talked about the weather and Mr. Johnson's prize tomatoes and cucumbers for a few minutes. Then Mimosa asked,

"Do you know any witches that I could talk to—light witches?"

Mr. Hempell chewed on the ends of his moustache and looked at Mimosa thoughtfully before answering. "Yes," he finally said. "I know one witch very well. Her name is Prunella. I will tell you how to find her. But since you are asking me, instead of your mentor, how to find a witch, I urge you to be careful of what you may be planning."

Mimosa sighed, and nodded. She really didn't need any more warnings or cautions today. "I will be careful," she told the gnome. "Please, I need your help."

Mr. Hempell told Mimosa where to find Prunella. Then he returned to his work. However, he glanced worriedly at his friend several times as he watched her walk away.

Mimosa chose a secluded spot behind a clump of trees in the park to change into fairy form. With a small *pop*, she transformed to her six-inch fairy self and flew quickly to a dense bit of woods where Mr. Hempell had told her Prunella lived.

She knocked on the door of the little wooden bungalow, and Prunella answered the door right away. "Hello," said the witch. "I don't have many fairy visitors. Come in, come in," she urged.

Prunella's house was very cozy. A number of fat, comfortable armchairs filled the main room; and the floor was strewn with brightly colored, hand-sewn rugs. The walls were lined with book-shelves, and a smooth oak table with four chairs occupied one corner.

Prunella herself was somewhat round and jolly. She wore a purple-flowered housedress, yellow slippers, and a necklace made of pumpkin seeds. Her gray hair was tied up in a bun. She also had pink cheeks and a bright dimply smile.

The witch was pouring tea and setting out cookies only seconds after Mimosa entered. Mimosa changed to her regular self to sit more comfortably in one of the fat armchairs, and to be able to have tea, since the cup and cookies would have been too large for a fairy to manage.

"So, what brings you here, dear?" asked Prunella, as she passed Mimosa a napkin.

Mimosa came straight to the point. "I'd like to obtain a stop-smoking seed from you."

Prunella didn't seem at all surprised by the request, but she did look keenly at Mimosa, who sensed that the witch knew *everything* about what the seed was wanted for, and what was going to happen to Mimosa because of her planned actions.

As she pulled down an old book from a high shelf in the corner, Prunella said, "I may be able to help you, but you should think carefully about what you are

doing. Mother Nature, Madam Toad, and your mentor will not know about this until the seed is actually used. But once the seed is consumed, the magic will be detectable and they will know immediately." With those words of advice, Prunella expertly flipped through the pages of her well-worn book.

"Yes," she said, after a few moments of flipping. "Here it is—The Stop-Smoking Seed. Let's see. Hmmm...yes, it involves 'waking willpower, addiction avoidance, serious sacrifice, and craving control.' We've already got the 'serious sacrifice,'" Prunella said slyly, giving Mimosa a very solemn look. "I can work on the rest of this and have the seed ready for you by tomorrow.

"I'll give you a list of herbs to collect for me," the witch added, "as a trade for the seed. That's usually how I get paid." Prunella then whipped out an already made-up list from the pocket of her dress.

Mimosa read the paper carefully through before leaving, to make sure she didn't have any questions. The list included basil, juniper berries, mint, thyme, sage, poppy seeds, and lilac petals.

"What spells or potions do you use these for?" Mimosa asked, interestedly.

"Oh no, dear," replied Prunella, grinning. "I don't use these for spells or potions. I use them for cooking, to make things tasty."

Mimosa smiled as she put the list in her pocket and changed back into her fairy self. They said goodbye and set a time the next day for the trade.

As soon as Mimosa got home, she sent a nut message to Periwinkle, to ask for her help the next morning. Periwinkle was the best fairy for tracking down edible plants.

When Periwinkle arrived the next day, the girls told Mrs. Welch that they would be taking a walk and playing in the park, and that they would be gone no more than two hours.

With Periwinkle's expert help, it didn't take them long to find everything. Mimosa wouldn't tell her friend what the herbs were for. She didn't want to get Periwinkle into trouble too. And she thought someone might try to stop her if they knew what she was planning.

Periwinkle went home early without trying to get further information out of her friend. She knew that she could never stop Mimosa anyway, once her mind was made up about something.

At the appointed time, Mimosa delivered the herbs to Prunella.

"Here it is, as promised," the witch said, handing Mimosa a small white paper envelope. The packet contained a single, tiny yellow mustard seed.

"You can add it to any type of food," said Prunella. "As long as the seed is consumed, it will work." Then she added, "But I put a spell on it. The seed cannot be used before Friday. That will give you a little extra time to think more about what you are planning to do, and what you will be giving up with this action."

Mimosa nodded, thanking Prunella, and turned to leave.

Chapter Four

Fairy Circle

Mimosa rode to Fairy Circle on Thursday with Madam Monarch and her niece, Marigold. When the fairies had gatherings, they usually met under trees that had special meaning to the purpose of their meeting. Today, they were meeting under a tall mulberry tree in the corner of a large, shady park. As they approached the tree, Madam Monarch told Mimosa and Marigold, "Mulberry trees are symbolic of great knowledge and wisdom."

The fairies were excited to welcome three new fairies to Fairy Circle today: Teasel, whose spirit was both a wildflower and an herb; Moonflower, who was pale and glowing white all over; and Madam Mariposa, whose butterfly wings were gray with yellow and orange accents.

Teasel and Moonflower were sisters, and Madam Mariposa was their grandmother and mentor. Teasel was seven and Moonflower was nine. They had just moved from Kentucky and were very happy to meet their new fairy friends. *Their* fairy handbooks were a light green color.

Spiderwort and Rosemary were especially happy to have Teasel join the group. For a long time, they had been the only herb fairies in the region. Though a lot of flowers were used as herbs, teasel flowers fell more into the herb category because of their useful qualities.

Mimosa went over to talk to Thistle, who was sitting by herself on a rock near the trunk of the mulberry tree. Thistle smiled

as Mimosa approached, but she was a dim version of her normally happy and bubbly self. She looked very tired.

Thistle's mother had given birth to baby sister Emily in the spring. This summer, Thistle had taken it upon herself to help her mother all she could. She had been helping with house cleaning, cooking, gardening, and caring for Emily. Even though her mother had not asked for this much help, Thistle wanted to make sure that her mother was able to get enough rest.

Also, Thistle liked spending a lot of time with her little sister. Emily had also been given a fairy spirit—that of a buttercup flower. Of course, Emily wouldn't learn about her fairy spirit for several years; but Thistle was very happy that she had something so special in common with her little sister.

Madam Robin was attending Fairy Circle today. She was Thistle's mentor, and in the future would also be assigned to mentor Buttercup. Madam Robin alone was unique among the fairy mentors because she was not a fairy. She was actually a robin, who had been bewitched many years ago to have long life and the gift of speech.

During the spring and early summer, Madam Robin had been unable to attend Fairy Circle because she was busy building a nest and raising a brood of baby robins.

Many of the young fairies ran to greet Madam Robin, hugging her as she twittered and sang to them with her beautiful bird-song voice. Everyone loved Madam Robin.

Mimosa happily visited with many of her fairy friends including Dragonfly, Tulip, Snapdragon, Dewberry, Cisthene, Morning Glory, Lily, and Firefly.

Most of the fairies were now able to approach Hollyhock on their own and speak to her easily by themselves. For several months, quite a few fairies in the group had been taking sign language classes so they could communicate better with Hollyhock. Primrose and Madam Swallowtail were both fluent in American Sign Language and usually interpreted for Hollyhock, but they didn't need to as often now because so many fairies were learning sign language.

The fairies all enjoyed refreshments that included powered sugar puff pastries, lemon jellybeans, datenut pinwheels, homemade fudge, raspberries, and peanut butter and marshmallow crème sandwiches. They also drank root beer and cool, sweet nectar from real honeysuckle blossoms. By the time Madam Toad called the meeting to order, the fairies were stuffed very full from the sweet-feast.

"We have another problem that needs our attention," said Madam Toad in her clear, strong voice. "The Spirit of Knowledge has requested our help to recover his niece.

She is the librarian for the Library of the Ages, which is part of the River of Wisdom. Apparently, the librarian was lured away by the Spirit of Ignorance, and we must find a way to get him to release her.

"You will probably want to look up a few things in your handbooks to have a better understanding of these matters," Madam Toad added. "But first, let me tell you who will make the journey. I have decided that Mimosa will lead this mission. Spiderwort and Dewberry will accompany her, and Madam Monarch will supervise."

Spiderwort was the fairy gifted with cleverness, quick thinking, and problem solving abilities. She had tall blue wings and a dress made of long green spiderwort leaves with bright blue flowers scattered over it. Her strawberry blond hair was pulled back in a headband covered with tiny spiderwort flowers, and she carried a bright red cardinal feather for her wand.

Dewberry's name was Lauren Kelley. She wore a dress made of creeping green vines with tiny black dewberries nestled among the crinkled leaves. She also had short black hair, small green wings, and a wand made from a single piece of braided unicorn tail hair. Dewberry's special fairy gift included great knowledge and wisdom. She knew legends, as well as facts, and was very much like a walking, talking set of encyclopedias.

Madam Monarch's special fairy gift involved great strength and endurance. She was also very majestic with tall, orange and black wings that flashed brilliantly in the sunlight. Her wand was a single, sparkling dandelion seed.

Madam Toad spoke again to give them their final instructions. "The Spirit of Knowledge was unable to come here to collect you because he is acting as librarian until his niece is returned, but he has sent his magic elevator to take you to him."

The fairies all looked at one another, questioningly. "I know," said Madam Toad, shaking her head. "I had never heard of a magic elevator before either, but it's waiting behind the tree trunk. After you consult your handbooks, the elevator will transport you to the River of Wisdom."

As Mimosa, Dewberry, Spiderwort, and Madam Monarch gathered together to look up things in their handbooks, the other fairies all trooped around the trunk of the tree to have a peek at the magic elevator. The elevator was square, about the size of a bowling ball box, and bright gold all over. Intricate carvings and odd symbols covered the top and sides of the golden box.

Dewberry went to say goodbye to her grandmother, and mentor, Madam Goldenrod, before joining the other fairies. "Why wasn't I chosen to lead the mission?"

she asked. "I am the fairy gifted with great knowledge and wisdom."

Madam Goldenrod was a little stern in answering Dewberry's question. "Yes, it is true that you are full of knowledge. However, true wisdom takes many years to develop. Mimosa's sensitivity and caring are much more potent and valuable at a young age. Understanding and caring are closely related to wisdom," the fairy mentor added. "You may actually lead the fairies one day, Dewberry, but only when your wisdom has developed to a much greater extent, with many years of life experiences contributing to it."

When Dewberry joined the others, they all sat in a circle, and Mimosa read the first relevant handbook entry aloud:

"The Spirit of Knowledge: Also known as Mage, the Spirit of Knowledge is overseer of the River

of Wisdom, which houses the Library of the Ages. A nymph works for him as librarian."

Mimosa looked up River of Wisdom next:

"*River of Wisdom:* The River of Wisdom is seven hundred and twelve miles long. It contains the Library of the Ages, which consists of all of the knowledge of mankind. The Spirit of Knowledge is in charge of the River of Wisdom, assisted by a nymph who acts as librarian."

"What exactly is a nymph?" asked Spiderwort. So Mimosa looked that up too:

"*Nymphs:* Nymphs are beautiful magical maidens inhabiting woods, rivers, mountains, seas, meadows,

 56

and trees. They are often employed by beings in positions of importance or power such as the Spirit of Knowledge. Nymphs age very slowly, like merpeople and satyrs, and can live for hundreds of years. Nymphs are believed to have the ability to capture unicorns, though that belief is not proven."

And finally, Mimosa looked up The Spirit of Ignorance:

"*The Spirit of Ignorance:* Also known as Dolt, the Spirit of Ignorance seeks to rid the world of knowledge and wisdom. He has the ability to lure others away from intellectual pursuits with the promise of ease, comfort, and bliss. He is very much like a salesman who peddles things like shortcuts, the

easy path, unearned prizes, useless
daydreams, forgetfulness, denial,
reality avoidance, apathy, selective
hearing, overindulgence, laziness,
and prejudice."

After Mimosa had finished reading, the mission participants said goodbye to Madam Toad and rounded the tree trunk to enter the golden elevator.

Madam Toad drove Marigold home, since it was going be awhile before Madam Monarch returned, and the distance would have been a long way for Marigold to fly by herself.

Chapter Five

The River of Wisdom

The magic golden elevator was a bit cramped inside. Madam Monarch and Spiderwort bumped wings trying to get situated. As soon as all four fairies had entered the elevator, the doors slid smoothly shut. The fairies never felt the elevator move. After what seemed like less than a minute, the doors slid open again, and they looked out onto a beautiful, sparkling river. Sunshine glittered brightly on the water's surface, winking at them.

The Spirit of Knowledge, looking very haggard and frazzled, ran to meet them.

He was the size of a regular person, had short gray hair, and wore long flowing purple robes. A soft glow covered his body, as though he were plugged in, like a night-light.

"Thank goodness you have come," the spirit said. "My name is Mage."

Mage somehow magically conjured up a small golden stool with a little wave of his finger, and sat himself down in front of the fairies before continuing. "I was very foolish," he said, shaking his head. "I saw the Spirit of Ignorance floating around the area two days ago, and I should have driven him off. But Dolt has never done anything like this before. He usually concentrates his attentions on regular humans.

"Sage is my niece," the spirit added. "She works for me as librarian. I admit I had a little too much elderberry wine yesterday, and I was very sleepy. I let my guard down. She was lured away sometime in the afternoon.

"Before we go on, let me show you the library." With this, Mage stood up and reached his hand deep into the pocket of his robe. He then tossed a handful of bright orange dust high into the air across the river. The cloud of dust flashed brilliantly for a second. In the area where the dust had passed, long rows of books, papers, and parchments appeared, but only for a few seconds.

"The library floats above the river," explained Mage. "It's invisible, of course. What would people think if they saw seven hundred and twelve miles of floating books, journals, scrolls, newspapers, tablets, letters, photographs, magazines, videos, and discs? The materials in the library are organized both alphabetically and chronologically, in two duplicate rows. When knowledge is needed, the

materials are delivered to mankind on the wings of swifts."

The fairies saw several swifts flying above the river, weaving and circling, obviously seeking out certain library items.

"When the information is no longer needed, the swifts return the reference materials to depositories all along the river. Sage is a master librarian, very organized and fast. She quickly files the items back into their proper places so they will be readily available for future use."

Then the Spirit of Knowledge asked, "Do you have any questions before I tell you how to begin looking for Dolt and Sage?"

"If the library contains knowledge," said Spiderwort, "why is the river called the River of Wisdom?"

"That is a very clever question," said Mage. "It is true that knowledge and wisdom are different. But knowledge is a part of wisdom. It is the root, base, and beginning of wisdom. As we progress through life, we develop wisdom from our experiences. This includes years of making decisions, recognizing mistakes, caring for humanity, developing tolerance, and learning to look at the 'larger' picture. Common sense and good judgment develop after many years of learning what to do with knowledge, and *that* is true wisdom."

None of the other fairies had any questions, so Mage went on. "The Spirit of Ignorance occupies many places. I usually see him lounging on large rocks along the edge of the river, or floating around in his house of straw. I know someone who may be able to help you find him. Come, let me introduce you."

The fairies accompanied Mage as he walked along the riverbank. His eyes scanned the water, looking for something. After a few minutes, he stopped and called out, "Ju-ju!"

About two seconds later, a large, shimmering fish jumped out of the water and hung suspended in mid-air in front of the fairies. He was a beautiful, bright orange color all over with a few black streaks and silver splotches. Ju-ju's fins and scales sparkled like shiny glass in the sunshine, and his large eyes were a deep amber color.

"Fairies! Hello! Hello!" Ju-ju shouted excitedly. The fairies all smiled and introduced themselves.

"Ju-ju was here when Dolt took Sage," explained Mage. "He is a friend of my niece, and he keeps an eye on the Spirit of Ignorance as often as possible."

"Two eyes, actually," said Ju-ju. "I will help you look for him. I think I know the travel patterns of his straw house."

Then Mage told them, "I wish you luck. I must get back to work." He bid them farewell, and returned to filing library materials in the absence of his librarian.

Chapter Six

Dolt and Sage

Ju-ju set off at once, not actually flying, but rather, swimming through the air. He talked happily to them as he swam. "I've never met a fairy before. I've seen fairies though, along the banks of the river."

The fairies did not feel the need to tell Ju-ju that they had never met a talking, air-swimming fish before. Instead, they just smiled.

"I am very sad about what has happened," Ju-ju said next. "Please, you must help get her back. Sage is my friend. If Dolt keeps her, she will be forced to work in his

School of Stupidity, helping him lure others into ignorance."

The fairies followed Ju-ju higher, above the clouds, to look for Dolt's house. After about an hour of flying, they spotted the gleaming house in the distance. The structure was perched on a puffy white cloud. The large house was made of glistening golden straw, airily woven together like a lacy basket.

There wasn't really a way to knock on the door, because a knock on straw wouldn't be heard. So Mimosa called out, "Hello! Is anyone home?"

A lazy voice answered from inside. "Come in."

The fairies all entered and held the door open for Ju-ju to go in as well.

The Spirit of Ignorance was also regular-people-size, like the Spirit of Knowledge. He sat in a large, turquoise-blue recliner, wearing a fuzzy green bathrobe and fluffy, bright pink slippers. His oversized chair was reclined as far back as possible, and his fluffy, pink-slippered feet stuck up high into the air.

The nymph sat in the corner of the room on a small stool very much like the one Mage had sat upon by the river. Sage was a very beautiful young woman. She had long, wavy red hair and soft gray eyes; and she wore a flowing, silvery-green dress. Sunlight poked its way through the walls of the straw house to shine on her dress and hair. Sage didn't say anything. She just looked at them, troubled and sad.

The only other furniture in the room was a large wooden table with a decanter of wine and a crystal goblet sitting upon it.

Ju-ju air-swam to the corner to be with Sage, while the fairies approached

Dolt. "Well, well," he drawled. "So many at once, I'm not losing my magnetism at all."

"We were not lured here," said Mimosa. "We've been looking for you."

"Well then, what can I do for you?" the spirit asked smoothly, yawning.

"The librarian must be returned to the River of Wisdom," replied Mimosa. "She is greatly needed." After pausing for a moment, Mimosa then asked, "Will you release her?"

"Oh, I'm afraid I can't do that," answered Dolt, with another yawn. "She came willingly, you see."

Spiderwort spoke next. "I see you have some boysenberry wine on your table. Would you like us to pour you a glass?"

"Well, that's very nice of you," Dolt replied. "Yes, thank you, I will have a glass."

Spiderwort remembered what Mage had said about drinking too much wine and letting his guard down. She was hoping for a similar result with Dolt. She pulled the stopper out of the glass decanter, while Madam Monarch raised her wand to put a spell on the heavy decanter and goblet so the fairies could lift them. "*Lighten*," she said, as a thin stream of golden light spewed from the tip of the gleaming dandelion seed.

With the *Anti-Gravity Spell* in place, Madam Monarch and Dewberry were able to easily pour the wine and carry the goblet to Dolt.

He thanked them graciously, and after a few sips said, "*Ahh...I needed that.*"

Mimosa perched on the arm of the recliner and smiled at the Spirit of Ignorance. Spiderwort, Dewberry, and Madam Monarch sat together on the edge of the table, waiting. And Ju-ju stayed in the corner with Sage to keep her company. The nymph never spoke. She just hung her head sadly.

After three full goblets of boysenberry wine, Dolt began talking to Mimosa about all of his woes. His voice was a little whiny because he was feeling very sorry for himself, and his words were a bit slurred because of the wine. But since Mimosa was a very good listener, he was happy to open up and let his troubles all pour out to her.

The spirit talked about how upset he was with all of the emphasis put on education these days, and children learning to read at younger ages, and more people than ever going to college, and how slow his business had been in recent years.

Mimosa listened calmly, nodding and sympathizing with him. "These kinds of changes must be very frustrating for you to experience," she said.

Dolt nodded, happy that someone could understand his challenges. He continued to vent his frustrations to her, and she continued to listen and nod.

Over an hour later, when the spirit was just about talked out, Mimosa said, "Well, I can see how much you've struggled, and how hard this has been for you. But the Library of the Ages is in such a mess without the nymph; she is desperately needed to sort it out. Is there anything that can change your mind about releasing her?"

Dolt's eyes glittered and he perked up a little, temporarily forgetting his woes. He sat forward in his recliner and rubbed his hands together, like he was about to make a deal. "What about a trade?" he suggested. "A beautiful fairy would be nice to keep me company. Any one of you would do," he said, glancing over at Dewberry, Spiderwort, and Madam Monarch.

Mimosa responded quickly. "Unfortunately, we are not just fairies; we are also girls. We have families and responsibilities, and we would be missed. None of us can stay with you."

Dolt looked a little gloomy after she said this, so Mimosa added, "Would you like anything else?"

With this, Dolt perked up again. "Well, I'm actually kind of hungry," he said. "I could trade her for some food, I guess."

Mimosa looked over at Madam Monarch, Spiderwort, and Dewberry, who all looked back at her. Then they looked at each other, rather bewildered.

After a very long pause, the three fairies at the table jumped up and began to plan an elaborate menu of food for Dolt. Mimosa continued to keep him company while Madam Monarch instructed Spiderwort and Dewberry on various *Food Creating Spells* to perform with their wands.

Barely twenty minutes later, the table was loaded with a delicious feast that included roasted chicken, barbequed spareribs, broiled steak, buttered ears of corn, mashed sweet potatoes, five kinds of pickles, steamed asparagus, creamy dilled zucchini, various breads, macaroni salad, two pies, a cobbler, and some homemade peanut brittle.

The fairies were actually having a lot of fun. Dewberry laughed, as she told her friends, "You're going to love this one." Pointing her wand, she gave it a little squiggle in mid-air, and said, "*Blackberry preserves.*" As a small puff of black smoke burst from her glistening white wand, a tiny jar of blackberry jam appeared, and Dewberry added, "Dewberries are part of the blackberry family."

A few moments later, Dolt rose from his recliner and shuffled his pink-slippered feet over to the table. He thanked the fairies, released the nymph, and settled himself in a chair to enjoy his feast.

The fairies didn't have time worry about how to get the nymph down from

the house in the clouds because Ju-ju informed them, "Sage can fly. The enchantment to fly is part of her job since the library floats above the river. She can swim too," he added happily. "We swim together all the time."

As the fairies, Sage, and Ju-ju flew away from the straw house, Spiderwort said, "That was almost too easy."

"Well, he's not very smart," replied Dewberry, "being the Spirit of Ignorance."

As they flew back to the river, Sage told the fairies, "I am very embarrassed. It was just so easy to follow him. I can't believe I was that stupid."

"Everyone makes mistakes," Mimosa told her. "We just have to learn from them and go on."

"Well, I have definitely learned my lesson," the nymph said. "I will never fall into that trap again. It's important to do what is right, not just what is easy."

Mage was overjoyed to see his niece and hugged her tightly. The spirit and the nymph both thanked the fairies several times for their help.

Ju-ju swam around them, expressing his happiness too. "Yes! Thank you! Thank you, fairies!"

The magic elevator transported the fairies back to the mulberry tree; and Madam Monarch drove Spiderwort, Dewberry, and Mimosa home in her lime green station wagon.

As she dropped Mimosa off last, Madam Monarch gave her a big hug, telling the young fairy, "Very good job today."

Mimosa smiled, and sighed, as she said goodbye to her mentor. She didn't watch as Madam Monarch pulled away, or look back to give a final wave goodbye. She had already made her decision, and it would not do to regret it beforehand, or make herself miserable by hanging on as long as possible.

Chapter Seven

The Second
Fairy Circle

Mimosa got up very early the next morning and sent Periwinkle a nut message that she had composed the night before. After giving the pecan to a friendly bluebird that often delivered fairy messages for her, Mimosa gazed out of the window for a few moments, watching the bird fly away.

In less than a minute, the bluebird became a small speck in the distance, barely visible against the pale turquoise sky.

Mimosa put on her robe and went into the kitchen. She filled two bowls with her favorite cereal, and took the tiny mustard seed out of

its paper packet. Then, using a toothpick, she poked a little hole into a piece of cereal and carefully placed the mustard seed inside. Her mother joined her just as Mimosa was pouring milk on the cereal.

By the time they had finished having breakfast, Alexandra was no longer a fairy, and she had no memory of ever having been a fairy.

Madam Toad called a special Fairy Circle for Sunday morning. The atmosphere was very subdued, because many of the fairies already knew that they had lost Mimosa. They met under a red oak tree. Oak trees could see the future and were very old and wise. Each fairy was given a beautiful peach colored candle to light as a tribute to their friend.

Madam Monarch addressed the fairies first. "As many of you know, Mimosa is no longer with us. Alexandra is just fine, but she no longer has a fairy spirit. She made a choice to relinquish it in order to help her mother stop smoking. I'm sure this was a very difficult decision for her.

"This part is very important," Madam Monarch added. "When any of you see Alexandra in the future, please remember not to discuss any fairy information with her. Since she has no memory of being a fairy, this would confuse her. If she found out she was once a fairy, it would probably sadden her greatly to realize what she has lost."

"Can't Mother Nature make an exception," asked Primrose, her voice shaking, "since Alexandra actually did a good thing?"

Madam Monarch shook her head sadly. "It is a firm rule. There are no exceptions, even for a good cause."

"I wish there was some way for her mother to know what her daughter sacrificed for her," added Lily. Several other fairies nodded in agreement.

Periwinkle addressed the fairies next, reading a note from Alexandra:

"'I am very sorry that I did not get to say goodbye to you all in person. I will miss you very much. Please, don't be sad for me. I made this choice, and I am fine with it. I will still have a good life, even though it will be a life without fairy magic. And I will still see many of you at school and Girls Club, so I am not losing you completely, though I know you will not be able to share fairy secrets with me. I believe there will be some memory of all of this in my heart, even though it will be removed from my mind.

Love,

Alexandra'"

Then Madam Monarch spoke again to the group. "I know we will all miss her very much. But we have been given a rare glimpse into the future with the help of Mother Nature and this oak tree. There

I am very sorry that I did not get to say goodbye to you all in person. I will miss you very much. Please don't be sad for me. I made this choice, and I am fine with it. I will still have a good life, even though it will be a life without fairy magic. And I will see many of you at school and Girls Club, so I am not losing you completely, though I know you will not be able to share fairy secrets with me. I believe there will be some memory of all of this in my heart, even though it will be removed from my mind. Love,
~Alexandra

are some things we can tell you about Alexandra's future life. Some good does come from this. Her mother will never smoke again.

"Alexandra *does* become a counselor. During a very long career, she has a positive impact on many others, contributing greatly to their lives.

"Also," said Madam Monarch, "Alexandra Hastings was born with a personality that is sensitive, caring, and understanding of others. These things were already ingrained in her personality, aside from her fairy spirit, so she has not really lost her gift.

"And I am pleased to tell you that there is another mimosa fairy in our region. She is only two years old, so she will not find out about her fairy spirit for several years. When she does join our group, we will tell her about the first Mimosa and her sacrifice. Alexandra's handbook and wand have both requested to be assigned to the new Mimosa. They will be kept safe for her until the time when she becomes aware of her fairy spirit.

"Finally, Alexandra's mother will remarry in the near future. She will have a second daughter who will also be blessed with a fairy spirit. When the time comes for her to join us, we will make sure that she knows her sister's story."

The fairies sat together quietly for some time, many of them hugging each other and crying. They would all miss Mimosa, but they also admired Alexandra's decision and were happy for her.

Chapter Eight

A Beginning

This had been a great weekend so far. Alexandra and her mother had spent most of Saturday shopping, running errands, taking a walk, playing Scrabble, and watching television together.

Sunday morning arrived, beautiful and bright, as Alexandra and her mother sat talking at breakfast. This was the third day in a row that Mrs. Hastings had not had a craving for a cigarette. She was extremely happy and proud of herself. "Something must have kicked in," she said, "maybe the hypnosis."

Alexandra was also very happy about this; and she felt proud too, as though she had helped in some way.

They talked for a long while together. The big discussion was about buying a house. Mrs. Hastings had been saving for a long time for a down payment on a house. Next month, they were going to start looking. If everything went as planned, they would be in the house by Christmas, or possibly even Thanksgiving.

Alexandra decided to take a walk to the park by herself later in the morning. As she was leaving, she helped herself to some golden raisins from a large box in the kitchen. Then she took a handful of lemon jellybeans out of an enormous canister and put them into her pocket to take with her. She had no idea why she liked golden raisins and lemon jellybeans so well. They were just really yummy. She also had a craving this morning for a

peanut butter and marshmallow crème sandwich. But she would have to wait until lunchtime for that.

On the way to the park, Alexandra passed a mimosa tree and paused. This was the prettiest tree on Evans Street. Her mother thought so too. In fact, they were planning to plant a mimosa tree in the yard of their new house. Delicate blossoms glinted in the sunlight, and the fernlike leaves rippled with the breeze. Alexandra breathed in the peachy smell of the blossoms, and smiled, as she continued on her way to the park. The sun was behind her and she enjoyed watching her shadow, dancing in front of her, almost as though it were leading her along on an important journey.

As she walked, Alexandra thoughtfully fingered the tiny sliver box on the chain around her neck. For some reason, there were warm, good feelings associated with the box. She couldn't remember when she had gotten this necklace, or who had given it to her. It must have been long ago, when she was very young. Maybe her father had given it to her. It was very comforting to hold the box in her hand. The necklace made her feel protected and safe.

In the park, Alexandra noticed several swifts overhead, flying around on what looked like extremely important business. One of the birds dipped very low, and his golden-brown eyes glinted at her as he passed.

Alexandra was very happy as she sat in a swing and watched other children playing, while the swifts swooped busily by. School would be starting tomorrow, and she was looking forward to it. She had thought a lot about her future lately, and she wanted to work very hard in school to be able to get into a good college.

On the way home from the park, Alexandra had the strangest urge to say hello to a watering can in Mr. Johnson's yard. The feeling was so strong that she stopped for a moment, peering closely at the aluminum can. This was certainly odd.

As she walked along, Alexandra pondered her summer. She used to dread the end of summer and going back to school. This year, the end of summer seemed like a good thing. For Alexandra, it was a beginning.

The End

Fairy Fun

Dewberry Interviews Ju-ju

Dewberry: Where were you born?
Ju-ju: In a magical lily pond in the garden of a giantess.

Dewberry: How did you learn to air-swim?
Ju-ju: From a library book about birds and planes.

Dewberry: Was it hard to learn?
Ju-ju: The first time was really scary because I got air up my nose. Then I remembered I was a magical fish and could breathe air, so I was okay after that.

Dewberry: What do you like to eat?
Ju-ju: Watermelon, cheesy crackers, and worms.

Dewberry: What are your favorite things to do?
Ju-ju: Blow bubbles and look for fairies.

Dewberry: Why do you like fairies so much?

Ju-ju: Because they are pretty and kind, and they can fly!

Dewberry: What is your favorite kind of art?

Ju-ju: Watercolor paintings. (Ju-ju sighs.) I love watercolors.

Dewberry: What kind of music do you like?

Ju-ju: Handel's *Water Music*.

Dewberry: Do you have any advice for our readers?

Ju-ju: Drink water instead of soda. It's better for you.

Your Own Interview

Using Dewberry's interview of Ju-ju as an example, try interviewing a friend or family member. You can learn a lot about someone just by asking some simple questions. In fact, you may learn something you never knew before! Here are some sample questions to get you started, but try coming up with some on your own. The key to a good interview is to ask questions that require more than a "yes" or "no" answer. For example, instead of asking, "Do you like fairies?" ask, "Why do you like fairies?" You will get an answer that is much more fun and interesting!

When is your birthday?

Where were you born?

If you had a fairy spirit, what would your fairy name be?

What is your favorite color?

What is your favorite sport?

Do you play a musical instrument? Which one?

What are your secret talents?

What is your favorite food?

What is your favorite book?

Which fairy would you most like to meet in person?

What is your favorite kind of music?

No Smoking Please

Mimosa was willing to give up her fairy spirit to help her mom quit smoking. Mimosa knew how dangerous smoking can be to a person's health, as well as to the environment. Smoking kills 4.8 million people worldwide every year. It can affect a person's heart, lungs, and brain. Smoking cigarettes can cause heart disease, heart attacks, and cancer. It even causes loss of hearing and vision, arthritis, bad breath, yellow fingernails, yellow teeth, wrinkles, and much more. Second-hand smoke can be just as harmful.

In addition to damaging a person's body, cigarette butts can harm the environment. Many people throw their cigarette butts on the ground instead of in proper waste collection bins. The butts eventually end up in sewer drains, which lead out to lakes and seas. People should not litter, but of course the best solution would be to not smoke at all!

Make a poster to encourage people to quit smoking or to tell kids why they should never start smoking. Visit your local library or search the internet to find out more facts about cigarettes and their dangers. Then get a large piece of paper or poster board to make your poster. You may decide to just write a message on it, or you may wish to draw pictures or cut some out of magazines to decorate it (but remember to get your parents' permission first). When you are finished, ask an adult where you can hang the poster so that others can see it.

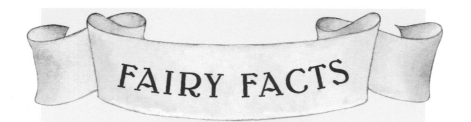

FAIRY FACTS

Long Rivers

The longest river in the world is the Nile in Africa at over 4,100 miles in length. The Amazon River of South America is second longest at right around 4,000 miles. And China has the third longest river, the Yangtze, which is over 3,900 miles in length.

The Largest River

The Amazon may be second as far as length, but it is certainly the largest river in the world carrying more water than the next six largest rivers combined. The source of the Amazon is a mountain in Peru called Nevado Mismi. The river travels through many South American countries including Brazil, Colombia, Bolivia, and Ecuador, and empties into the Atlantic Ocean. Like all rivers, the dynamics of the Amazon change throughout the year. During the rainy season, the river can reach depths of over one hundred feet and widths in some places of twenty-five miles. The river is home to many species of wildlife including anacondas and piranhas.

Elevators

Mimosa and her friends use a magic elevator to get to the River of Wisdom. Many people use elevators every day to get to their classrooms, their jobs, or even their homes. What you may not know is that elevators have been around for a long time! In fact, some believe the first (very primitive) elevator was invented in 236 B.C. by the Ancient Greek mathematician Archimedes. The elevator as we know it today was invented in the 1850s and was powered by steam. The first electric elevator came about in the 1880s. Today's inventors work to create even better versions of the original elevators, making elevators safer and faster. In fact, the world's fastest elevator is in Taipei's Taipei 101 building and can take you from the fifth floor to the eighty-ninth floor in only thirty-seven seconds!

Taipei 101 building

Inside you is the power to do anything

The Fairy Chronicles

. . . the adventures continue

Cinnabar and the Island of Shadows

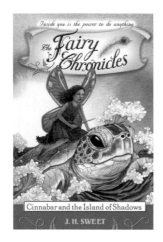

A shadow is a person's closest companion. Shadows protect and guide the humans they are attached to. But what if you were born without a shadow?

Madam Toad paused before she continued. "Human shadows are unlike any other shadows on earth. They are much different from animal, mountain, plant, cloud, insect, and building shadows. For starters, human shadows are much more complex. And they are the only shadows that are magically constructed. Human shadows are manufactured by shadowmakers on the Island of Shadows, and are delivered to children shortly after their births by hawks that work for the shadowmakers."

"Today, Mother Nature has discovered that seven children in various countries of the world have not received their shadows."

And so Cinnabar, Mimosa, Dewberry, and Spiderwort must travel to the Island of Shadows, confront the King and Queen of that remarkable place, discover what happened to these seven shadows, and, worst of all, find out if there might be someone or something behind it all!

Come visit us at fairychronicles.com

Primrose and the Magic Snowglobe

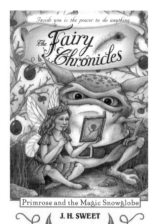

Primrose and the Magic Snowglobe

J. H. SWEET

Burchard the gargoyle has just been fired from his job guarding a church from evil spirits because he can't stop walking around, Ripper the gremlin is fixing things instead of breaking them, and Mr. Jones the dwarf is telling people his own name and spreading dwarf secrets to non-dwarves. What is wrong with these people?

When Madam Toad had everyone's attention, she spoke more solemnly. "By now, many of you may have guessed why our visitors are here. It is unusual for a gargoyle to move around, for a gremlin to enjoy fixing things, and for a dwarf to reveal secrets. As far as anyone can tell, these are recent and singular occurrences among gargoyles, gremlins, and dwarves. Burchard has been fired from his job. Ripper has been driven out and is being pursued by other gremlins. And Mr. Jones has been banished by the dwarves.

"We have no idea how these things occurred," Madam Toad continued, "and a reason why must be found so that things can be put to right."

Primrose, Luna, and Snapdragon are put on the case, with the help of Madam Swallowtail. Interestingly, all three of the magical creatures remember making a wish and seeing a man with a snowglobe. Could it really be that the Wishmaker has returned? Primrose must use her detective abilities to solve the mystery.

Come visit us at fairychronicles.com

Luna and the Well of Secrets

Three bat fairies have been kidnapped and taken to the Well of Secrets. To make matters worse, the Well of Secrets is the doorway to Eventide, the Land of Darkness!

"There must be extremely powerful magic involved to snatch fairies from three completely different parts of the world all in one day."

Madam Toad's face wore a puzzled expression as she continued. "And the reason only bat fairies were abducted is unknown..."

Luna, Snapdragon, Firefly, and Madam Finch are sent to the Well to discover why. Once there, they discover a Dark Witch imprisoned in a mirror, only able to come out for twelve minutes every twelve hours. Then a Light Witch arrives and the fairies have to make a choice. Who do they trust? Which one is good and which one is evil? Will they defeat the right witch without destroying the balance between light and dark?

This may be the most dangerous fairy mission ever!

Come visit us at fairychronicles.com

The adventures
don't end here!

Come visit us at
www.fairychronicles.com

for even more
fairy magic
and fun!

- Become a Fairy Chronicles member
- Upload your own fairy drawings
- Read about all of the *Fairy Chronicles* adventures—and get sneak peeks of the next books
- Meet each fairy and learn more about your favorite characters
- Help protect Mother Nature with cool recycling activities and ideas
- Check out the online Fairy Handbook as well as trivia, recipes, poems, and crafts
- Download special bookmarks, computer graphics, and more free stuff
- Send your friends *Fairy Chronicles* e-cards

And much more!

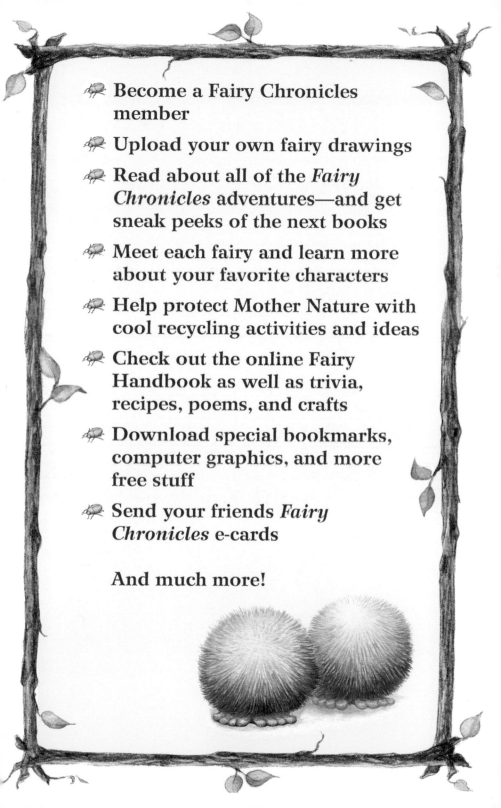

About the Author

J.H. Sweet has always looked for the magic in the everyday. She has an imaginary dog named Jellybean Ebenezer Beast. Her hobbies include hiking, photography, knitting, and basketry. She also enjoys watching a variety of movies and sports. Her favorite superhero is her husband, with Silver Surfer coming in a close second. She loves many of the same things the fairies love, including live oak trees, mockingbirds, weathered terra-cotta, butterflies, bees, and cypress knees. In the fairy game of "If I were a jellybean, what flavor would I be?" she would be green apple. J.H. Sweet lives with her husband in South Texas and has a degree in English from Texas State University.

About the Illustrator

Holly Sierra's illustrations are visually enchanting with particular attention to decorative, mystical, and multicultural themes. Holly received her fine arts education at SUNY Purchase in New York and lives in Myrtle Beach with her husband, Steve, and their three children, Gabrielle, Esme, and Christopher.